Copyright © 2022 Clavis Publishing Inc., New York

Visit us on the Web at www.clavis-publishing.com.

Try, Try Again written by Adam Ciccio and illustrated by Azize Tekines

ISBN 978-1-60537-7292

This book was printed in June 2022 at Nikara, M. R. Štefánika 858/25, 963 01 Krupina, Slovakia.

First Edition
10 9 8 7 6 5 4 3 2 1

Clavis Publishing supports the First Amendment and celebrates the right to read.

Written by **Adam Ciccio**
Illustrated by **Azize Tekines**

Try, Try AGAIN

Clavis
NEW YORK

I want to ride my BIKE,

but I just **LEAVE** it be.

I rode it once before,

but crashed and scraped my knee.

It's boring in my room.
I shouldn't have to hide.

I want to join my friends.
If only I could ride!

I tell myself I'll fall
and get too hurt to play.
But friends say they fell too,
got up, then rode away.

I focus on the **BAD.**

My brain's been feeling **STUCK**.

But riding looks like **FUN**.

It's time to change my **LUCK!**

I'll push aside my fears—
find courage; yes, I must!
I'm sick of hanging back,
just left out in the dust.

Okay, I'll get back on . . .

leave worry in the past.

I pedal slow at first,
but soon I'm spinning fast!

I race down all the hills
and cruise around the bend.

I learned my lesson well:
You must try . . .
THEN TRY AGAIN!